Caillou

Goes To Work

Adaptation of the animated series: Roger Harvey
Illustrations taken from the animated series

Caillou was going to Mommy's office for the first time. He was very proud to be using his new backpack.

"Careful, Caillou! Those are revolving doors. Let me help you," said Mommy.

"I can do it myself!" Caillou replied.

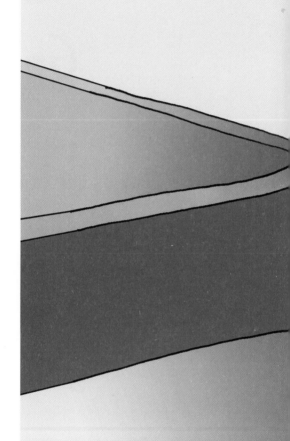

The elevator was full of people
Caillou didn't know. He raised
his head and looked around.
A man smiled at him. At last,
the elevator doors opened.
"Hello, Caillou," said the
receptionist.
"Caillou is here to work,"
Mommy said.

"Wow!" Caillou exclaimed when he saw Mommy's office.
"Look, you have your very own desk," Mommy said.
She helped Caillou take off his backpack and jacket.

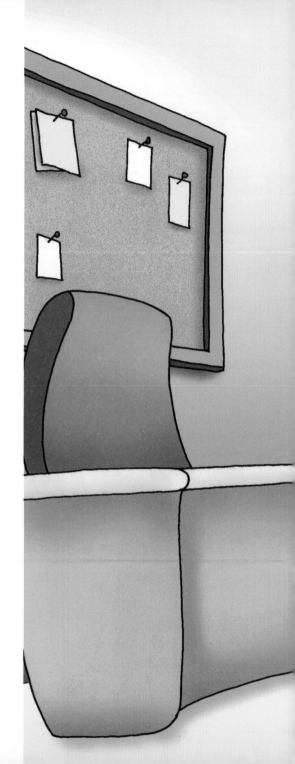

Caillou sat in the big chair behind the desk.
Mommy sat down at her computer.

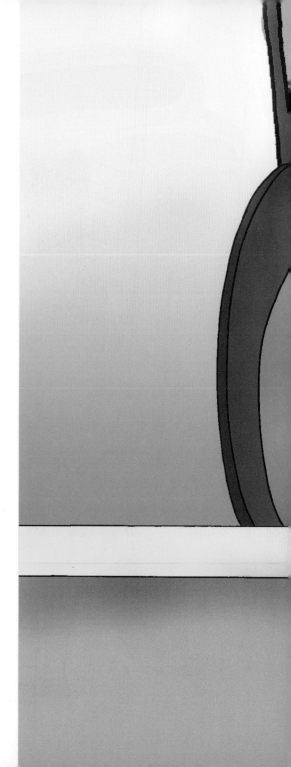

Looking very serious, Caillou opened his backpack and took out some paper and crayons. He drew a head, body, legs. "Finished!" Caillou exclaimed. "Look, Mommy! That's you, there's Daddy, that's Rosie, and this is me." "That's wonderful, Caillou."

"I want to play with you,"
Caillou said.
"I've still got a lot of work to
do. Why don't you draw a
picture of Gilbert?"
asked Mommy. Caillou went
back to his desk. Then Caillou
remembered his teddy bear in
his backpack.
"You know, Teddy, Mommy's
work takes a long time,"
Caillou said with a sigh.

Mommy came over to Caillou's desk, picked up the phone and dialed a number. "It's for you," she said. Surprised, Caillou took the receiver.
"Hello? Daddy? It's me, Caillou. I'm working with Mommy. Yes, I'm doing work too. I love you, Daddy. Bye."

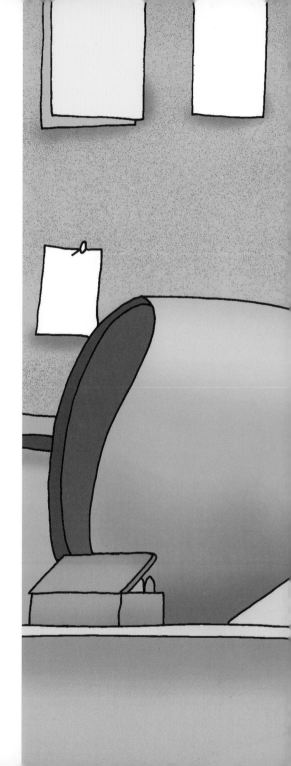

"It's lunchtime, Caillou. Are you hungry?" Mommy asked.
"I'm starving!" Caillou replied.
For lunch, they had a ham and cheese sandwich, cookies, an apple and some juice. Caillou loved eating in the office.
It was like a picnic!

"Why don't we hang up your picture?" Mommy suggested.
"Oh, yes! I'll do it," said Caillou.
Caillou was so busy hanging his picture on the wall that he didn't hear Daddy come in.
"Good for you, Caillou! Your drawing is great!"
"Daddy!" cried Caillou.

Mommy helped Caillou put on his jacket and backpack.
When they left the office, Caillou walked in front of Daddy. He liked being able to show the way.

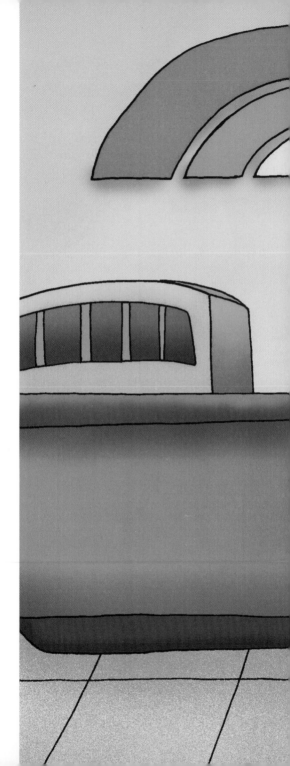

"Look, Daddy, revolving doors."
"You sure know a lot," Daddy
replied.
"Wait! I'll show you how they
work," said Caillou. He went to
the door and pushed firmly.
On the way home, Caillou told
Daddy all about his first day at
work.

Text: adaptation by Roger Harvey of the animated series CAILLOU,
produced by DHX Media Inc.
All rights reserved.
Original story written by Marie-France Landry
Illustrations taken from the television series CAILLOU and adapted by
Les Studios de la Souris Mécanique.
Art Direction: Monique Dupras

The PBS KIDS logo is a registered mark of PBS and is used with permission.

Chouette Publishing would like to thank SODEC and the Government of Canada
for their financial support.

Québec
Books
Tax Credit

Gestion
SODEC

Canada

Bibliothèque et Archives nationales du Québec and Library and Archives
Canada cataloguing in publication

Harvey, Roger, 1940 -
Caillou goes to work
New ed.
(Clubhouse)
Translation of: Caillou va travailler.
Originally issued in series: Backpack Collection. c1999.
For children aged 3 ans up.

ISBN 9782894509067

1. Work - Juvenile literature. 2. Work environment - Juvenile literature. I. Title
II. Series: Clubhouse.

HD4902.5.H3713 2012   j331   C2011-942189-5

Printed in China
10 9 8 7 6 5 4 3 2 1 CHO1953 AUG2015